For Jeremy —
Love,
Lucy

Copyright 1992 by Toy Works Press
Illustrations Copyright 1992 by Lucinda McQueen
All rights reserved under International
  and Pan-American Copyright Conventions.
Published in the United States by
Toy Works Press, Middle Falls, New York 12848

Library of Congress Cataloging in Publication Data

  Burgess, Thornton W. 1874-1965

PETER RABBIT PLAYS A JOKE

Summary: Out for a walk with Johnny Chuck, Peter Rabbit
  plays a joke which backfires.

1. Fantasy — Fiction   I. McQueen, Lucinda, ill.

II. Title

Library of Congress Catalog Card Number 91-075207
Series 1 Number 2

ISBN 0-938715-05-4
Printed in Singapore
Published January 1992
First Printing

This book was typeset in Goudy Old Style.

Editor: Edward Dowling
Designer: Catherine Wagner Minnery
Art Director: John Gunther

Peter Rabbit
Plays
A
Joke

By Thornton W. Burgess
Illustrated by Lucinda McQueen

One morning when big round Mr. Sun was climbing up in the sky and Old Mother West Wind had sent all her Merry Little Breezes to play in the Green Meadows, Johnny Chuck started out for a walk. First he sat up very straight and looked and looked all around to see if Reddy Fox was anywhere about, for you know Reddy Fox liked to tease Johnny Chuck.

But Reddy Fox was nowhere to be seen, so Johnny Chuck trotted down the Lone Little Path to the wood.
Mr. Sun was shining as brightly as ever he could and Johnny Chuck, who was very, very fat, grew very, very warm.

By and by he sat down on the end of a log under a big tree to rest.
Thump! Something hit Johnny Chuck right on the top of his round little head. It made Johnny Chuck jump.

"Hello, Johnny Chuck!" said a voice that seemed to come right out of the sky. Johnny Chuck tipped his head way, way back and looked up. He was just in time to see Happy Jack Squirrel drop a nut. Down it came and hit Johnny Chuck right on the tip of his funny, black little nose.

"Oh!" said Johnny Chuck, and tumbled right over back off the log. But Johnny Chuck was so round and so fat and so roly-poly that it didn't hurt him a bit.

"Ha! Ha! Ha!" laughed Happy Jack up in the tree.
"Ha! Ha! Ha!" laughed Johnny Chuck, picking himself up. Then they both laughed together, it was such a good joke.

"What are you laughing at?" asked a voice so close to Johnny Chuck that he rolled over three times, he was so surprised. It was Peter Rabbit.

"What are you doing in my wood?" asked Peter Rabbit.

"I'm taking a walk," said Johnny Chuck.

"Good," said Peter Rabbit. "I'll come along too."

So Johnny Chuck and Peter Rabbit set out along the Lone Little Path through the wood. Peter Rabbit hopped along with great big jumps, for Peter's legs are long and meant for jumping, but Johnny Chuck couldn't keep up, though he tried very hard, for Johnny's legs are short.

Johnny Chuck promised to be very, very still, for he wanted very much to see what Peter Rabbit had found. Peter Rabbit tiptoed down the Lone Little Path through the wood, his funny long ears pointing right up to the sky. And behind him tiptoed Johnny Chuck, wondering and wondering what it could be that Peter Rabbit had found.

Johnny Chuck tried to jump very high and very far,
just as he had seen Peter Rabbit jump, but Johnny Chuck's
legs are very short and not meant for jumping. Besides,
Johnny Chuck was very, very fat.

So, though he tried very hard indeed to jump just like Peter Rabbit, he stubbed his toes on the top of the mossy green log and over he tumbled, head first, and landed with a great big thump right on Reddy Fox, who was lying fast asleep on the other side of the mossy green log.

Peter Rabbit laughed and laughed until he had to hold his sides.

My, how frightened Johnny Chuck was when he saw what he had done! Before he could get on his feet he had rolled right over behind a little bush, and there he lay very, very still.

Reddy Fox awoke with a grunt when Johnny Chuck
fell on him so hard, and the first thing he saw was Peter
Rabbit laughing so that he had to hold his sides. Reddy
Fox didn't stop to look around. He thought that Peter
Rabbit had jumped on him. Up jumped Reddy Fox and
away ran Peter Rabbit.

Away went Reddy Fox after Peter Rabbit. Peter dodged behind the trees, and jumped over the bushes, and ran this way and that way just as hard as ever he could, for Peter was very much afraid of Reddy Fox. And Reddy Fox followed Peter behind the trees and over the bushes this way and that way, but he couldn't catch Peter Rabbit.

Pretty soon Peter Rabbit came to the house of Jimmy
Skunk. He knew that Jimmy Skunk was over in the pasture,
so he popped right in and then he was safe, for the door
of Jimmy Skunk's house was too small for Reddy Fox to
squeeze in.

Reddy Fox sat down and waited, but Peter Rabbit didn't come out. By and by Reddy Fox gave it up and trotted off home, where old Mother Fox was waiting for him.

All this time Johnny Chuck had sat very still, watching Reddy Fox try to catch Peter Rabbit. And when he saw Peter Rabbit pop into the house of Jimmy Skunk and Reddy Fox trot away home, Johnny Chuck stood up and brushed his little coat very clean.

Then he trotted back up
the Lone Little Path through
the wood

to his own little path through
the Green Meadows, where
the Merry Little Breezes
were still playing,

till he was safe in his own
snug little home once more.